Note to parents, carers and teachers

Read it yourself is a series of modern stories, favourite characters and traditional tales written in a simple way for children who are learning to read. The books can be read independently or as part of a guided reading session.

Each book is carefully structured to include many high-frequency words vital for first reading. The sentences on each page are supported closely by pictures to help with understanding, and to offer lively details to talk about.

The books are graded into four levels that progressively introduce wider vocabulary and longer stories as a reader's ability and confidence grows.

Ideas for use

• Although your child will now be progressing towards silent, independent reading, let her know that your help and encouragement is always available.

• Developing readers can be concentrating so hard on the words that they sometimes don't fully grasp the meaning of what they're reading. Answering the puzzle questions on pages 46 and 47 will help with understanding.

For more information and advice on Read it yourself and book banding, visit www.ladybird.com/readityourself

Book
Band
9

Level 4 is ideal for children who are ready to read longer stories with a wider vocabulary and are eager to start reading independently.

Special features:

Clear type

Full, exciting story

Richer, more varied vocabulary

Then one day, a stranger went to see the mayor. He was dressed in red and yellow. In his hand he carried a pipe.

"I am the Pied Piper," said the stranger, "and I can make the rats go away."

18

19

Longer sentences

Detailed illustrations to capture the imagination

The mayor said, "If you can make these rats go away, I will give you lots of money."

"Very well," said the Pied Piper. "But don't forget your promise."

Then the Pied Piper went into the streets of Hamelin and began to play a strange tune.

20

21

Educational Consultant: Geraldine Taylor
Book Banding Consultant: Kate Ruttle

A catalogue record for this book is available from the British Library

Published by Ladybird Books Ltd
80 Strand, London, WC2R 0RL
A Penguin Company

002

© LADYBIRD BOOKS LTD MMX. This edition MMXIII
Ladybird, Read It Yourself and the Ladybird Logo are registered or
unregistered trademarks of Ladybird Books Limited.

ISBN: 978-0-72327-321-9

Printed in China

The Pied Piper
of Hamelin

Illustrated by Tamsin Hinrichsen

Once upon a time,
there was a beautiful
little town called Hamelin.

The people of Hamelin were
all very happy, until the day
the rats came.

Thousands of rats came to Hamelin. There were big rats and little rats, thin rats and fat rats. There were rats in all the houses and rats in all the shops.

"There are rats on my table!"
said one man.

"There are rats under my chair!"
said another.

"There are rats in my kitchen!"
called one woman.

"There are rats in my bed!"
called another.

"There are rats all over the house!" called a little boy.

"Make these rats go away!" called a little girl.

The people of Hamelin
went to see the mayor.

"Get rid of these rats!"
they shouted.

"What can I do?" said the mayor.
"There are rats in my house, too.
I can't get rid of them."

But the people said, "You must make all the rats go away. If you don't make them go away we will choose another mayor."

Then one day, a stranger went to see the mayor. He was dressed in red and yellow. In his hand he carried a pipe.

"I am the Pied Piper," said the stranger, "and I can make the rats go away."

The mayor said, "If you can make these rats go away, I will give you lots of money."

"Very well," said the Pied Piper. "But don't forget your promise."

Then the Pied Piper went into the streets of Hamelin and began to play a strange tune.

21

The rats heard the tune and stopped what they were doing.

Suddenly, one rat ran after the Pied Piper. Then another rat ran after him. And another. Soon, all the rats ran after the Pied Piper.

23

The Pied Piper walked towards the river, still playing the strange tune on his pipe.

The rats followed him and jumped into the river. And that was the end of the rats.

The Pied Piper went back
to see the mayor.

"The rats have all gone,"
he said. "Please give me the
money you promised me."

"No," said the mayor. "I have
no money to give you."

"If you don't give me the money," said the Pied Piper, "I will play another tune, and you will not be so happy then."

"You can do what you like," said the mayor.

So the Pied Piper went out into the streets and began to play another tune.

In all the houses and in all the streets, the children stopped playing. Then, one by one, they ran after the Pied Piper.

The people of Hamelin called
to the children to stop, but
the children didn't hear. They
followed the Pied Piper through
the streets and over the river.

33

They followed the Pied Piper out of the town and up a mountain.

Suddenly, the mountain opened up and the Pied Piper went inside. The children followed him. Inside the mountain was a beautiful land full of trees and flowers and birds.

But one little boy had hurt his leg
and he couldn't keep up with the
other children. He saw his friends
go into the mountain, but he was
too late to follow them.

The little boy went back to the town and went to see the mayor.

"My friends are inside the mountain with the Pied Piper," he said. "They will never come back."

The people of Hamelin were
very unhappy.

"Where are our children?"
they shouted to the mayor.
"You must go and find them."

So the mayor went to look for
the children. He looked for
years and years and years.
He is still looking
for them now.

How much do you remember about the story of The Pied Piper of Hamelin? Answer these questions and find out!

- What is the problem in Hamelin?

- Which colours is the Pied Piper dressed in?

- How does the Pied Piper get rid of the rats?

- Why is the Pied Piper so cross with the mayor?

- Where does the Pied Piper take the children?

- Who goes to look for the children?

Unjumble these words to make words from the story, then match them to the correct pictures.

melhani   stra   iped priep

yomar   linchred   tinmuudon

Read it yourself with Ladybird

Tick the books you've read!

For more confident readers who
can read simple stories with help.

Level 3

 YOU won't like this present as much as I DO!

 The Elves and the Shoemaker

☐ ☐

 Hansel and Gretel

 Harry and the Bucketful of Dinosaurs

 Jack and the Beanstalk

 Furi on Music Island

 Poppet Stows Away

 Rapunzel

 The Red Knight

☐ ☐ ☐ ☐ ☐ ☐ ☐

Longer stories for more independent,
fluent readers.

Level 4

 I am Inventing an INVENTION

 Harry and the Dinosaurs United

☐ ☐

 Heidi

 Katsuma and the Art Thief

 Luvli and the Glump-a-tron

 The Pied Piper of Hamelin

 Sam and the Robots

 Snow White and the Seven Dwarfs

 The Wizard of Oz

☐ ☐ ☐ ☐ ☐ ☐ ☐

 Available on the App Store

The Read it yourself with Ladybird app
is now available for iPad, iPhone and
iPod touch

App also available on Android devices